To my three little engines, Carlin, Rory, and Andie—
always remember the journey
—BM

For all people who act for greater, equitable
good and say, "I know we can . . ."
—LF + SJ

GROSSET & DUNLAP
An Imprint of Penguin Random House LLC, New York

Visit us online at www.penguinrandomhouse.com.

Library of Congress Control Number: 2020002223

ISBN 9781524793357   10 9 8 7 6 5 4 3 2 1

The Little Engine That Could®

THREE LITTLE ENGINES

written by Bob McKinnon
illustrated by Lou Fancher and Steve Johnson

Grosset & Dunlap

Graduation day was finally here!
The three little engines were excited
to take their final test of Engine School:
making their first solo trip over the mountain.

On the other side of the mountain, their teacher, the Rusty Old Engine,
waited to greet them with their friends and family.

Each engine took their place on a different track,
waiting for their turn to be called.

On Track 1 whistled
the cheerful and plucky
Little Blue Engine.

On Track 2 puffed
the fast and confident
Yellow Passenger Engine.

And finally, on Track 3 chugged the strong
and fiery Red Freight Engine.

The stationmaster called to the Little Blue Engine,
"You're up first. Are you ready?"

"Yes, ma'am!" she replied, and off she went.

The sun was shining brightly as the Little Blue Engine rounded
a few bends and continued toward tall green pine trees.
When she came to the steepest part of the mountain,
she wondered whether she could make it to the top.

Up, up, and up the Little Blue Engine climbed,
chugging, "I think I can, I think I can, I think I can."

And before she knew it, she did!
Merrily, she puffed down the mountain,
reaching the village without any trouble.

The Rusty Old Engine met her at the bottom of the hill.
"Congratulations!" he said. "You made it."

Everyone in the village cheered,
and her lights beamed brighter than they ever had before.
She was so proud that her hard work had paid off.

Back at the train terminal, the stationmaster called
to the Yellow Passenger Engine, "Are you ready?"

"Yes, ma'am!" he bellowed, and off he went.

The journey on Track 2 had more twists and turns. He snaked sharply around big boulders and rumbled over bumpy ground.

As a passenger engine, he was pulling lots of cars behind him. He made it up over several smaller slopes, chugging, "I think I can, I think I can, I think I can," but he grew very tired by the time he got to the steepest stretch near the top of the mountain.

Dark clouds began to cover the sun.
Then suddenly, strong winds and heavy rain
started to blow the Passenger Engine back.

As he tried to push forward, he chattered,
"I, I, I, think, think, think, I can, can—can't."
He could not go another inch.

Exhausted, he stopped in his tracks,
smoke slowly sputtering from his stack.

The Red Freight Engine, who had been waiting anxiously to follow her friends, was now up. "Are you ready?" called the stationmaster.

"Yes, ma'am!" she chugged, and off she went.

Her journey on Track 3 had a much steeper path to the top of the mountain. She traveled up and down the many slopes, chugging loudly, "I think I can, I think I can, I think I can," the whole way.

As a freight engine, she was pulling cars that were filled with big, heavy machines, and when she came to the steepest stretch of all, she had to puff and puff her way up the mountain. But looking off into the distance, she could see something was in her way.

As she got closer, she realized that
a large tree had fallen on her track.

With the Red Freight Engine's path blocked,
she came to a full stop. The village seemed so near,
but she could not push past the fallen tree. Hissing softly,
the Freight Engine sadly realized, "I cannot graduate now."

In the village, the Little Blue Engine waited for her friends.
She wondered what was taking them so long.

She called out, "What's the matter? Why did they stop? Did they quit?"

The Rusty Old Engine came up beside her and said, "They aren't
quitting. Maybe they have gone as far as they can go right now."

The Little Blue Engine was confused. "But I made it here. Why can't they?"

The Rusty Old Engine smiled. "Close your eyes and think back on your journey. How many twists and turns were there on your track?"

"A few."

"Did you face wind and rain?"

"No," she said. "The sun was shining and
I guess there was a little wind at my back."

"How many steep stretches
did you have to climb?"

Counting in her head,
she remembered, "Just the one."

"How heavy was your load?"

A little embarrassed, she said quietly,
"Well, I wasn't asked to pull any other cars."

"Was there anything blocking
your track?"

"No, it was clear."

"But I did work hard to
get over the mountain, though.
I thought I could, I thought
I could, and I did."

"Of course you did,"
the Rusty Old Engine agreed.

The Little Blue Engine sat quietly
for a moment, thinking about how
her journey might be different
from that of her friends.

And then a little light went on in her heart.

"My friends worked really hard, too. But they got stuck.
Just because you think you can, doesn't always mean you will, does it?"

"No, it doesn't," replied the Rusty Old Engine.

"Some engines make it here, and others have things
that get in their way—no matter how hard they try,"
continued the Little Blue Engine. "I wonder,
is there anything we can do to help them?"

Smiling at each other, the two engines chugged,
"I think we can, I think we can, I think we can."

And so they did.

Over the hills . . .

Into the rain . . .

And past the trees . . .

Until, finally, all three engines came rumbling down the mountain.

The End